Dear Parents and Educators,

Welcome to Penguin Young Readers! As parents and educators, you know that each child develops at his or her own pace—in terms of speech, critical thinking, and, of course, reading. Penguin Young Readers recognizes this fact. As a result, each Penguin Young Readers book is assigned a traditional easy-to-read level (1–4) as well as a Guided Reading Level (A–P). Both of these systems will help you choose the right book for your child. Please refer to the back of each book for specific leveling information. Penguin Young Readers features esteemed authors and illustrators, stories about favorite characters, fascinating nonfiction, and more!

## The Tale of Peter Rabbit

LEVEL **2**

GUIDED READING LEVEL **I**

This book is perfect for a **Progressing Reader** who:
- can figure out unknown words by using picture and context clues;
- can recognize beginning, middle, and ending sounds;
- can make and confirm predictions about what will happen in the text; and
- can distinguish between fiction and nonfiction.

Here are some **activities** you can do during and after reading this book:
- Character Traits: In this story, Peter Rabbit is described as "a naughty, little rabbit." Make a list of other words that can be used to describe him.
- Make Predictions: At the end of the story, Peter Rabbit is put to bed. What do you think he will do when he wakes up the next morning? Discuss how you would continue the adventures of Peter Rabbit.

Remember, sharing the love of reading with a child is the best gift you can give!

—Bonnie Bader, EdM
  Penguin Young Readers program

*Penguin Young Readers are leveled by independent reviewers applying the standards developed by Irene Fountas and Gay Su Pinnell in *Matching Books to Readers: Using Leveled Books in Guided Reading*, Heinemann, 1999.

Penguin Young Readers
Published by the Penguin Group
Penguin Group (USA) Inc., 375 Hudson Street, New York, New York 10014, USA
Penguin Group (Canada), 90 Eglinton Avenue East, Suite 700, Toronto, Ontario M4P 2Y3, Canada
(a division of Pearson Penguin Canada Inc.)
Penguin Books Ltd., 80 Strand, London WC2R 0RL, England
Penguin Group Ireland, 25 St. Stephen's Green, Dublin 2, Ireland (a division of Penguin Books Ltd.)
Penguin Group (Australia), 250 Camberwell Road, Camberwell, Victoria 3124, Australia
(a division of Pearson Australia Group Pty. Ltd.)
Penguin Books India Pvt. Ltd., 11 Community Centre, Panchsheel Park, New Delhi—110 017, India
Penguin Group (NZ), 67 Apollo Drive, Rosedale, Auckland 0632, New Zealand
(a division of Pearson New Zealand Ltd.)
Penguin Books (South Africa) (Pty.) Ltd., 24 Sturdee Avenue,
Rosebank, Johannesburg 2196, South Africa

Penguin Books Ltd., Registered Offices: 80 Strand, London WC2R 0RL, England

Visit our website at: www.peterrabbit.com

Color reproduction by Saxon Photolitho.

*Library of Congress Cataloging-in-Publication Data is available.*

ISBN 978-0-7232-6815-4

# The Tale of Peter Rabbit

based on the original tale by Beatrix Potter

Penguin Young Readers
An Imprint of Penguin Group (USA) Inc.

This is Peter Rabbit.

He lives here with his mother,

Mrs. Rabbit, and his sisters,

Flopsy, Mopsy, and Cotton-tail.

One morning Mrs. Rabbit said,

"I am going out, children.

Now run along, but don't go into

Mr. McGregor's garden."

Then Mrs. Rabbit picked up
her basket and her umbrella.
She walked through the woods.

Flopsy, Mopsy, and Cotton-tail

were good little rabbits.

They went to pick berries.

But Peter was a naughty little rabbit.

He ran to Mr. McGregor's garden and squeezed under the gate!

Peter sat in the garden and ate
lots of radishes.

Then, feeling sick, he went to
look for some parsley to make
himself feel better.

He went around the corner.

# And met Mr. McGregor!

Mr. McGregor ran after

Peter Rabbit.

He waved a rake and shouted,

"Stop, thief!"

Peter ran into a net and got

caught by the buttons on his

blue jacket.

Then Mr. McGregor tried to
trap Peter.

Peter wriggled out.

But he lost his jacket and shoes.

Peter jumped into a watering can to hide.

Mr. McGregor was looking for him.

He looked under all the flowerpots.

Then Peter jumped out of

a window.

He knocked over some

flowerpots.

And he got away!

Mr. McGregor was tired of

running after Peter.

He went back to work

in his garden.

Peter heard the **scritch**, **scratch**

of Mr. McGregor's hoe.

He climbed up to look across

the garden.

He could see the gate!

Peter ran as fast as he could.

Mr. McGregor saw him but Peter didn't care.

He slipped under the gate and was safe at last.

When Peter got home,

he was so tired!

He flopped down on the floor.

Mrs. Rabbit was cooking.

"Where have you been,

Peter Rabbit?" she asked.

Peter Rabbit was not feeling well.

Mrs. Rabbit put him to bed and

made him some tea.

But Flopsy, Mopsy, and
Cotton-tail had bread and milk
and berries for dinner.